W9-DGX-746

Strange but True Auto Racing Stories

by Al Powell

SCHOLASTIC BOOK SERVICES

NEW YORK • TORONTO • LONDON • AUCKLAND • SYDNEY • TOKYO

For Betty Ruth, who understood me
during the better days and stood by me
during the difficult ones.

Cover Photo by Stanley Rosenthall/DeWys

Photo Credits: pp. 8, 11, 21, 29, 46, 52, 66, 78, 83 (top and bottom),
88 (top and bottom), Indianapolis Motor Speedway; p. 3 (top) Key-
stone View Co., p. 3 (bottom) Courtesy of the Ford Archives, Henry
Ford Museum, Dearborn, Michigan.

ISBN: 0-590-09880-2

This book is sold subject to the condition that it shall not be resold,
lent, or otherwise circulated in any binding or cover other than
that in which it is published — unless prior written permission has
been obtained from the publisher — and without a similar condition, including this condition, being imposed on the subsequent
purchaser.

Copyright © 1974 by A. H. Powell, Jr. All rights reserved. Published by
Scholastic Book Services, a division of Scholastic Magazines, Inc.

13 12 11 10 9 8 7 6 5 4   0 1 2/8

Printed in the U.S.A.   11

Contents

Acknowledgments

I am deeply grateful to the many persons who have helped me with this book and who have given so generously of their thought and labor. The omission of any name indicates an unsystematic, but not ungrateful, author.

My thanks to Dorothy Asendorf, Charlotte, NC; Al Bloemker, Indianapolis, IN; Bobby Day, Miami, FL; Vern "Flip" Fritch, Riverview, FL; Bob Gegen, Miami, FL; Peter Helck, Millerton, NY; Bobby Johns, Miami, FL; Mrs. Richard Losenbeck, Opa Locka, FL; Dennis May, *Automobile Quarterly Magazine*; Len Milde, Lorain, OH; Junior Palmer, Lake Worth, FL; M. C. "Shorty" Pritzbur, Philadelphia, PA; Dick Rogers, Miami, FL; John G. Sawyer, Sarasota, FL; Pat Singleton, Pace Management Corp., Houston, TX; Don Sobol, Miami, FL; John Suiter, Lumberton, NC; Al Sweeny, Tampa, FL; Henry Tillman, Charlotte, NC; and Bill Wilcox, Miami, FL.

Henry Ford's Wildest Ride

Henry Ford, speed-merchant.

Does that sound strange?

The sober withdrawn man who founded the Ford Motor Car Company is not remembered as a daredevil, yet he broke a world's speed record — in the dead of winter under hair-raising conditions.

At the turn of the century, the automobile was merely a "summer toy." Demand for cars dropped with the first frost and stopped with the first snow.

Since Ford could not sell his cars during the winter months, he switched to a sideline — speed. Racing cars were important to the infant auto industry for their publicity value.

During the winter of 1903-4, Ford and a few

helpers worked on a racer, the Arrow. It was the twin of Ford's 999, which Barney Oldfield had driven to the 1903 national championship.

Ford wasn't satisfied. He wanted a world's speed record. He reworked the racer in his Detroit factory till it was more powerful and faster than the 999. He called it the *new* 999.

Ford watched nearby Lake St. Clair. As winter wore on, the lake froze over. It seemed the ideal race course. When the ice became firm enough to support the car, Ford contacted the American Automobile Association. Officials were sent to time the run.

All was ready by January 12, 1904. A three-mile straightaway had been scraped clear of snow and spread with cinders to afford the tires a bit of traction. The timing committee inspected the course and set up the needed standards — flags, flagmen, and timers. Ford rolled the new 999 from the shed.

His crew used blowtorches to heat the big engine. Once started, it roared and rumbled. The carburetor expert, Spider Huff, adjusted the fuel mixture.

An official gave Ford the signal to start. He climbed to his seat and gripped the two-handled bar that steered the brutish machine. Spider Huff got aboard also. He crouched on a tiny platform beside the engine, where he could operate the carburetor adjustments while underway.

Henry Ford stands beside one of his early racing cars, with Barney Oldfield at the "wheel."

Ford in the driver's seat of the car he drove to a new land speed record — over ice. His mechanic, Spider Huff, clings to the side.

Ford engaged the clutch and the racer leaped forward.

As the 999 picked up speed, the smooth-looking ice began to take on fiendish characteristics. Although level to the eye, it was rough and ribbed to the hurtling car.

The bouncing was so fierce Ford could not keep his foot on the gas pedal. Huff had to maintain speed. He used one hand to hold the throttle wide open, and clung to his perch with the other.

Half the time the 999 seemed to be in the air. Twice it slithered completely off the cinder path. Ford muscled it back and raced on toward the finish.

Seconds later the 999 roared between the end stands. Official watches clicked. The time was a new speed record! Ford had clocked 39 and 2/5 seconds for the mile run. His speed of 91.37 miles per hour was exactly 6.64 mph faster than the existing record.

Considering the conditions of cold, wind, and a treacherous track, it was an amazing feat. The crew shouted with joy.

But out on the ice, things were far from joyous.

Ford was trying to stop. He had fought the racer from the start to keep it accelerating and heading straight. Now he had to bring the big car to a stop on the frozen lake.

Reducing throttle, he gently applied the brakes.

The car responded by swerving from side to side. From his perch beside the engine, Spider Huff could do nothing but hold tight and pray.

Both men feared for their lives. Directly ahead loomed the hulk of a large icebound lake schooner, the *Garibaldi*. Skidding and seemingly out of control, the 999 was heading right for the sturdy beams of the ship!

Ford kept his head and eased off the brakes. Slowly he turned the tiller bar to the side. The 999 swung gently toward the shore line. At the last instant it skidded past the ship's bow and slammed to a stop in the snow on the shore.

Miraculously neither Ford nor Huff was hurt. They had flown through the air and landed in a soft bed of snow. The onlookers rushed over to congratulate them. Ford and Huff were limp and exhausted. They could manage only the feeblest of smiles.

So ended a fantastic run. Henry Ford, founder of the Ford Motor Car Company, went into the record books as the first man to drive an automobile over land at more than 90 mph.

But he actually did it over water — and nearly crashed into a ship parked on the course!

Fisher's Folly

Carl Fisher was a millionaire with a cause. He wanted to prove that Americans could build better race cars than the Europeans.

The first International Vanderbilt Cup race was to be held on Long Island, New York, on October 8, 1904. Fisher made up his mind to enter an American-made car, one that could whip the cocky foreigners.

He went to The Premier Motor Car Company of Indianapolis, Indiana, and explained what he wanted. Never mind the price. Never mind the appearance. The car had to be fast and sturdy, a cross between a gazelle and a grizzly bear.

At a cost of $15,000, he got what he asked for —

a monster. The car looked awful. But its gigantic four-cylinder, air-cooled engine drove it faster than 70 mph; the engine probably could have done as well in a locomotive.

The delighted Fisher forgot the ugliness and the cost. He filed early for the race.

But the race officials did not immediately accept the entry. Instead they asked for detailed information on the car. They also enclosed a copy of the Vanderbilt Cup race rules, which caused Fisher to choke on his cigar. Cars acceptable for the race, he read, had to weigh less than 2,204 pounds. Weight had never entered his mind!

When he recovered from the shock, he rushed to The Premier Motor Car Company to trim some poundage off his hulking contender. Every piece of nonessential equipment was thrown out. The racer was stripped to the bare frame and rolled onto the scales. It had to be lightened further. But with nothing left to take out except the driver's seat, Fisher ordered something put in. Holes!

The drilling went on for hours. In all, 474 holes, ranging from a half inch to one and a half inches, were bored in the frame rails, in the engine supports, and in the stout axles. One more hole and the car might have fallen apart.

The riddled giant was rolled onto the scales again. It was still 200 pounds overweight. Fisher stomped out in a purple rage.

Although the Premier never did line up for the Vanderbilt Cup it did race once. On November 4, 1905, it won a local handicap event on an oval track, turning the final lap in 59 mph, a respectable speed for racers of the era.

Today it stands in the splendid Indianapolis Speedway Museum. Visitors know it as the "Swiss Cheese Racer" and have fun counting the holes.

The "Swiss Cheese Racer" in the Indianapolis Speedway Museum.

Model T at Indy

The Model T Ford, built between 1909 and 1927, was the backbone of early auto transportation in America.

A rugged simple car, it delighted owners by turning them into mechanics. With a pair of pliers, a screwdriver, and some wire, repairs could be made without professional help.

The little four-cylinder engine was so easy to fix that even the worst fumbler felt justified in dreaming of a higher calling: namely, racing.

Few owners made it, but many of their cars did. After years of faithful family service, a good many Model T's were reborn as racers. Modified, and known as Ford Specials, the T became "king of the dirt tracks."

Loyal supporters insisted the T had the power and stamina to compete anywhere, including the yearly 500-mile race at Indianapolis. Eventually, the T's began showing up at the big track, and did well.

In 1923 a T averaged 83 mph around the Indy track and finished fifth. Fans gave it the biggest cheer of the day as it crossed the finish line. Thousands of men in the crowd, with T's of their own parked behind the grandstand, saw themselves at the wheel, their dreams of glory come true.

The 1930 event also had its share of T-Ford entries. One had been reworked by Arthur Chevrolet, whose brother had designed the first Chevrolet automobile.

Arthur Chevrolet's T was to be driven by a young man from the dirt track circuits, Chet Miller. In time, Miller would rank with the leading drivers in the nation. In 1930, he was just another rookie trying to finish in the money.

Chevrolet checked the speed of other entries. He believed his car, #41, had a real chance. His instructions to Miller were simple: Maintain an average speed of 100 mph. The last four Indy races had been won at speeds below the century mark. Chevrolet felt that the car averaging 100 would win.

Gradually the field loosened up. Cars began to

Chet Miller at the wheel of the Ford Special that raced at Indy with a borrowed front spring from one of the cars in the parking lot.

slow down or drop out with mechanical trouble. The T was running strongly.

On the 92nd lap (230 miles), Miller brought #41 in for fuel, tire check, and carburetor adjustment. He was preparing to return to action when he was stopped. A technical inspector pointed to a cracked front spring.

The T could not resume the race until the spring was replaced!

What to do? The crew had a good supply of spare parts, but no extra front spring. Chevrolet could think of only one possible solution.

He sent two mechanics into a nearby parking lot to "borrow" a front spring from an unattended Model T passenger car!

When they returned, the broken spring had been removed from Miller's car. The borrowed one was installed, and Miller was allowed to reenter the race.

He drove as fast as possible to make up for the time lost. When the race ended, he had worked his way back up to 13th position, in the 28-car field.

But for the long pit stop to replace the spring, the T might have won. Chevrolet was right to hold Miller at the 100 mph speed. The winner, Billy Arnold, took the flag at an average of 100 mph in that 1930 race!

As for the borrowed spring, it was replaced. But as the owner of that passenger car came down from the grandstand and drove home, his mind probably still whirled with the sounds of the growling motors and whining rubber. Chugging down city streets, he was for a few minutes more a lean and tireless, begoggled speed-merchant tearing around the great track in his Model T.

His imagination betrayed him, for the truth was more fantastic. He was in fact driving a car that, in part, had been there!

No Peanuts in the Pits!

Race drivers are a superstitious lot. One of their strangest fears concerns the humble peanut.

Peanuts are always sold in the grandstands. That's okay. But they just don't belong in the pit area.

Does that sound nuts?

Not if you are a racing car driver. Or if you were in Nashville, Tennessee, in late September of 1937, for the American Automobile Association Championship Class races.

As the drivers and crews in that race were waiting for the program to begin, one of the younger mechanics walked into the pit area. He was eating peanuts.

"Hey, Mac," a white-haired crew chief shouted.

"Get away from here with those peanuts. Don't you know they bring bad luck?"

"Plain foolishness," the peanut-eater scoffed.

And to prove his point he contemptuously broke peanut shells over the hoods of the first five cars in line.

Angry crewmen, brushing off the shells, silently cursed the young wise guy.

In due course the heats were called and then the semifinals. The wheels of the powerful cars stirred up the track, and with each race the hard-packed clay surface became more dusty.

The 25-lap final got underway in a low-hung haze. Duke Nalon, the track record holder, took the lead. He was still ahead when the flagman held five fingers above his head. Five laps to go.

Nalon raced toward the turn just as a slower car lost control and spun completely around. It disappeared in a cloud of billowing yellow dust.

Unable to see where the spinning car had gone, Nalon tried desperately to slow down. The rest of the onrushing field followed him into the dense cloud.

Fans heard the sickening crunch of shattering wood, the shrieks of metal tearing and crumpling, the screams of pain. Then all was quiet. The dust settled.

Woody Cox, whose spin had started the chain reaction, lay in the dirt. Duke Nalon was slumped in his car, unconscious. Three other cars were wrecked.

Cox was dead. Nalon and the three other drivers, Ted Horn, Chet Gardner, and Vern Orenduff, were seriously injured.

Each man was driving one of the five cars over which the scoffing young mechanic had sprinkled peanut shells. Coincidence? Maybe, but that's how superstitions are born.

A basic dirt-track racer of the 30's: wire wheels, larger rear wheels (with knobby tires where allowed), outside exhaust pipe, no roll bars, flat steering wheel, outside handbrake lever, dirt-shaker screen on radiator, and formed pipe bumpers.

The Hands of Jim Hurtubise

Over the years he had been beating the best drivers in America. Now, after the crash, he lay in a hospital bed with critical burns.

His hands and face had taken the brunt of the flames. The fingers which had handled a steering wheel so well rested at his sides, unmoving, lifeless.

He lay on his back, eyes closed, his mind seeing into the future. He would race again. As soon as he recovered...

The doctors who had treated him knew differently.

His name was Jim Hurtubise, but everyone called him Herk. And if his doctors believed he would never drive again, they did not know what made Hercules tick.

Herk was born in North Tonawanda, New York, in 1932. Grown to manhood, he stood a sturdy five-feet-nine. He wore his hair cropped short in a crew cut that reflected his no-frills determination.

To get his start, he had driven anything on wheels and from the first he was hard on equipment. He would charge for the lead flat-out. If the car held together, Herk usually won.

He gained experience in the open-cockpit midget racers, tiny editions of the Indy racers of the day. Then he moved to California, where competition was stiffest, and began driving the more powerful sprint racers.

He made a name for himself as a "charger." An independent car owner with an eye for gutsy new talent signed him and Parnelli Jones, another future great, to compete in the big-time — in the United States Auto Club sprint car races.

These races were traditionally dominated by Indy veterans driving Offenhauser-engined cars. Herk and Jones were to challenge in cars powered by Chevrolet V8's.

Herk and Jones turned tradition upside down. They broke records, won any and all kinds of races, and started the V8 revolution that survives today.

Herk's fame grew, and in 1960 he was offered a

chance to drive in the Indianapolis 500. His car was not known for exceptional speed. During the trials, however, Herk turned in fast times by broadsliding the turns.

"You don't drive at Indy that way," veterans cautioned him.

Herk made his critics gag on qualifying day. He destroyed the track records. He set a new one-lap mark of 149.601 and a new four-lap average of 149.056!

During the race he ran with the leaders until a broken connecting rod forced him out. Nevertheless he was named Rookie of the Year for his performance.

A horseman jockey is known for his seat, and a racing car driver is known for his hands. Herk had the hands. Driving against the best in the USAC Championship Division in 1960, he set a mark by qualifying in every event scheduled that year.

He lived for driving and drove the year round. Although a star at any race, he was at his best at Indy. He led the race in 1961 and 1962 only to have mechanical mishaps deprive him of victory.

In 1963 Herk signed to drive one of the famous old Novi racers then owned by Andy Granatelli. The cars dated back to 1941 and were sentimental favorites of the fans. Granatelli's updated antiques had not been able to qualify for the 500 in the past four years. Even the most diehard Novi enthusiasts admitted that racing had passed them by.

No one had seen Herk behind the wheel of one, however. On the first day of qualifying he drove the antique faster than it had ever run before, 150.257 mph. It took a track record of 151.847 by Parnelli Jones, his old teammate and the eventual winner of the race, to nudge Herk from the pole position.

Herk started the race in the middle of the front row. In the trials he had come through for the old timers who knew the Novi could still run. In the race he did the impossible once again. He led the vital first lap, setting a record of 143.335 mph.

He was running second past the halfway mark when the Novi was black-flagged. Officials suspected the old car of leaking oil. Herk was waved out of the race.

After Indy, Herk went on a rampage, winning five straight events against top-flight drivers. A crash sidelined him for many months, and he spent his recovery period reworking a car for the next Indy 500.

He qualified, but once again engine failure — this time loss of oil pressure — sidelined him after 141 laps. Undaunted, he entered the car the following Sunday in an annual Indy-car race at Milwaukee, Wisconsin. It was June 7, 1964.

He was challenging for the lead when he went

into a spin. The car crashed, rupturing the fuel tank. Instantly he was enveloped in a deadly alcohol fire.

Firemen had the blaze out in seconds. They saved Herk's life, but his hands and face, unprotected by his fireproof overalls, were terribly burned.

He was flown to the military burn center at San Antonio, Texas. All that was medically possible was done. It was not enough.

Now he lay on his hospital bed, his thoughts reaching toward the day when he would again be gripping a steering wheel and charging for the lead.

Jim Hurtubise at the wheel of the Granatelli STP Novi V8 less than a year after his tragic accident.

The doctors did not know how to break the news. "Herk," one of them said uncomfortably. "Your fingers will never move again. We plan a final operation and, to get the most use of the fingers, we must know what you plan to do after you leave here."

Racing was Herk's life and all he planned to do.

"Shape 'em to fit a steering wheel," he said.

So Herk's hands were shaped to fit a steering wheel and he returned to racing.

You will see him at Indy. You will see him at the long-distance stock car races — the 500 milers at Daytona, Pocono, Michigan International, and other big tracks.

Herk is there, charging for the lead, his hands hooked rigidly about the steering wheel.

"That Girl Flies"

In the pioneer days of auto racing, promoters had to offer the crowds added attractions in order to fill their grandstands. It took quite a show to make a tight-fisted farmer part with his hard-earned cash and buy a ticket.

But when Elfrieda Mais competed, no added attraction was ever needed. Fans flocked to the track hoping to see the female driver upset the men.

Elfrieda was a novelty. Women drove in exhibitions and special events, she vied with the men in regular races. Elfrieda left many a dirt track driver behind, red-faced and fumbling for excuses.

Her husband, Johnny, was a driver-mechanic whose career dated back to 1912. He drove the small tracks and the large. In 1915 he took a whack at Indianapolis. Overheating forced him out early, and he finished twenty-second.

He returned to his true love, dirt track racing at midwestern county fairs. He prospered and built a second car, but finding a dependable driver for it was a continuous headache. More often than not, his second finished out of the money or embracing a fence post.

The day came when Elfrieda could hold her tongue no longer.

"I could do as well as those so-called drivers you hire, Johnny," she grumbled.

Johnny looked at her a moment and grinned.

"You know, you might at that," he said. "At least, it's worth a try."

Having hung around racers all her married life, Elfrieda had a foundation to build upon. Johnny gave her a briefing on track driving, then put her behind the wheel. He circled the track, with Elfrieda following. Mile after mile he guided her, slowly at first, and then faster and faster. By the end of the afternoon, she was keeping up at high speeds.

From that day on, Elfrieda was Johnny's team driver. She developed steadily until she was competing with the men on equal terms.

Johnny DePalma, a veteran driver witnessing one of her victories, exclaimed, "That girl flies!"

From 1922 until 1934, Elfrieda and Johnny toured midwestern tracks as the Mais Racing Team. Their popularity grew with every appearance.

Elfrieda asked no special favors in her races, and Johnny often bet the promoter that they could run one-two against the best drivers he had.

When not racing, the couple drove for an auto thrill show. They performed trick driving, precision stunts, and other crowd-pleasing acts. Elfrieda's good looks and daredevil showmanship made her a star.

Her glamour act was to ride a motorcycle through a flaming wall. The success of this dangerous feat depended upon Elfrieda's nerve and skill. She never faltered; it was a freakish movement of the flames that took her life.

The setting was the 1934 Alabama State Fair in Birmingham. The thrill show was a major attraction. Elfrieda sat on her rumbling motorcycle while the announcer introduced her and explained the perilous act. Then with a wave to the crowd, she raced around the fairground track, broadsliding through the turns in a breathtaking display of riding prowess. After a few laps she stopped her machine at the far end of the oval and acknowledged the cheers.

All was now ready for the wall crash. Elfrieda raised her hand as a signal to light the fire.

The crew had drawn a circle on the wall with gasoline, which, when lighted, would give her a target to ride at. If she rammed the center portion of the flame ring, she would hit the breakaway section of the wooden boards and pass through safely.

A match was tossed at the base. The flames leaped skyward. Elfrieda Mais began her last ride.

The fuel was burning fiercely as she raced around the track. Unnoticed by anyone, a gusty wind was blowing the flames to the side... past the breakaway boards. At full speed, Elfrieda rode toward a false target.

She hit the heavy beam framework of the wall, veered out of control, and crashed into a large road grader parked by the speedway. She was killed instantly.

Elfrieda Mais was 30, an age that normally allows many more years of competition. Had she lived, she might have been the first woman to break into big-time auto racing.

She had already proved her ability against men on the dirt tracks, where most of the name drivers got their starts. She was good, and in the last moments of her life she was too good. Every eye was trained upon her. No one wanted to miss a split second of the stunt. Had interest wavered, someone might have noticed the circle of flames creeping on its deadly course.

The Cornelian

The streamlined racers that whiz around the Indianapolis 500-mile track are a special breed.

Small and lightweight, they have neither frame nor axles. The wheels are attached to spindly springs, bars, and pivots. A strong aluminum body supports the engine, transmission, fuel tanks, and other parts.

These swift, nimble racers came to Indianapolis in the early 1960's from overseas, notably from England. In 1964 the three fastest entries were of this type. Americans hailed their design as revolutionary.

"Ultramodern, space-age racers," newspapers called them. Longtime auto observers claimed they had brought to Indy the first real change in design since the big speedway opened in 1911.

Was it so?

The answer lies half buried in the past.

More than 50 years before the perky English cars outran their rivals in 1964, there lived a man who manufactured auto parts in Kalamazoo, Michigan. His name was Harold Blood, and he had built a small car that he hoped to put on the market.

The car was different. It was small, like the English racers of the 1960's. It had no axles and no frame, like the English racers. And, like the English racers, it was lightweight and easy to handle.

But was it a racer?

It was not meant to be. Rather it was simply a low-priced runabout. Blood had built it using his own ideas — ideas unheard of in 1912, the year of his first model.

Blood knew he had built a good car. He named it Cornelian and managed to sell a few. But selling was not his line.

Then an opportunity to boost sales plopped into his lap. A race of one hundred miles around a dirt track was scheduled in Kalamazoo. The prize money attracted crack professional drivers. As a publicity stunt, Blood entered one of his Cornelians.

The little machine, with its modest 18-horsepower engine, was allowed to run though no one felt it had a chance. Not even Blood.

His goal wasn't to win. He hoped simply to demonstrate the car's ruggedness and reliability in the high-speed test. To finish without breaking down would be victory enough.

The Cornelian not only finished the 100 rough miles, it came in seventh. It beat nearly half the field of big, high-powered racers. The other drivers were stunned. What manner of car was this tiny upstart?

Blood was thrilled by the performance of his car. He decided to enter a specially prepared Cornelian in the 1915 Indianapolis race. If he could finish in the top ten, sales success was assured.

The famous engineer-driver, Louis Chevrolet, was hired to pep up the car and drive it in the race. The little roadster got a new look: tapered tail, oversized wheels, and reworked engine.

How well it was pepped up became clear at the Indy time trials. On the first day it was the only car capable of completing the required four laps at the qualifying speed.

The next day a Bugatti from France clocked 81.5 mph. The Cornelian had done 81.1 mph. The French racer housed an engine three times larger, and yet it had averaged only four-tenths of a mile per hour faster!

Blood kicked up his heels in joy.

The Cornelian with Louis Chevrolet, and mechanic wearing reversed cap in the traditional "racing style." The car had no front or rear axles. The wheels were supported by springs, as in modern racing cars, and the steering was by chain connection. A crank was needed as the car had no starter in racing trim.

When the big race got underway, Chevrolet was able to keep up with the pace fairly well. All went as planned until the engine broke a valve. After 180 miles, the Cornelian was retired.

Thus ended the brief fling of Harold Blood and his car of the future. What happened to it? Why was it never heard from again?

Success killed it.

Harold Blood's main business was Blood Brothers Manufacturing Company, which made car parts. Among the patents the company held was an advanced type of universal joint that had been used in the Cornelian.

Following the 1915 Indianapolis 500, the universal joint came into great demand. Other auto companies wanted it. After turning out a total of one hundred Cornelians, Blood discontinued building automobiles. He concentrated on manufacturing universal joints.

The years passed and Blood became wealthy. One by one his aging cars wore out. They were hauled to the junkyard and forgotten.

And yet there they were in the 1960's — spanking new racing versions brought by the Europeans to Indianapolis. Lightweight winners without axles or frames.

American experts called them the first major breakthrough in design since the opening of Indy. And why not? After half a century, who remembered the 1915 Indianapolis race and a curious little also-ran called the Cornelian?

"You Just Ran Over Floyd!"

The jewel of stock car oddities is a whacky accident that happened far from the eyes of spectators. The setting was the Medley Speedway in Miami, Florida. The date, June 14, 1952.

Phil Garrett, driver of the #47 car, had started the night well. His practice laps had been fast.

The car's owner-mechanic, Floyd Whitfield, smiled broadly as he clicked the last run with his stopwatch. Then he lifted his flashlight high and winked it.

Phil caught the signal and pulled into the pits.

"She feels strong tonight," he said.

Floyd held the watch out for Phil to read.

"Wow!" exclaimed Phil. "Look at that, will you!"

"We may make a few bucks if you keep out of trouble," Floyd said jokingly.

The lineup for the first heat was called. Phil started in the middle of a ten-car field. By expertly dodging a wild tangle, he took the checkered flag in second place.

"Heads up driving," Floyd said as Phil came in. "I thought you were a goner when those fellas spun in front of you."

Phil was fairly bristling with eagerness to get out on the track again. "She's really humming tonight," he said gleefully.

The car was checked over and made ready for the semifinals. The event was longer than a heat, and tougher because the field was larger. Even so, Phil finished second again.

Back in the pits he was greeted by Floyd's smiling face and a healthy slap on the back.

"She's great," said Phil happily. "One thing, though...take a look at the right rear brake. It seems to be hanging up a bit when it gets hot."

"I'll attend to it," Floyd said. "Go and get a cold drink. You look bushed."

"I'm gone," said Phil with a grin, and strode to the refreshment stand.

As he sipped his drink, the pit steward ran up. "Any of you dudes want to run this semi?" he asked. "I've got two out with engine problems, and I want to fill the field."

"Put me down," Phil answered eagerly. "I'll run anytime tonight."

"Crank up and get out there," the steward told him. "They're ready to start."

Phil dashed back to the car. He grabbed his helmet and jumped inside. He was whistling as he started the engine and drove off toward the gate.

What he did not remember was that Floyd lay under the opposite side of the car, repairing the brake assembly. The wheel rolled across Floyd's chest.

At the gate Phil stopped and waited for the "OK" to enter the track. Then he heard it.

"Phil! Phil!" a steward shouted. "You just ran over Floyd!"

Phil saw the emergency beacon begin to blink beside him. That meant one thing: "Send the ambulance — quick!"

Parked in the center of the track, Doc Davis saw the emergency beacon too. In seconds his rescue vehicle was racing to the pit area. But it was not Floyd who was destined to be carted to the hospital....

Phil unbuckled his harness and jumped from the car. He could see Floyd lying on the ground. He began to run. The impact of the situation hit him. "My best friend...I've killed him!" Phil fainted.

Doc Davis reached Floyd and knelt beside him.

The car owner moaned, "Oh, man...w-what happened?"

Doc waved a vial of smelling salts under his nose. "You OK, Floyd?" he asked. "Lie still while I check these ribs."

"I'm all right, Doc," gasped Floyd. "Got the wind knocked out of me, is all."

An ordinary passenger car would have crushed him. But the stock car, stripped of fenders and every ounce of unnecesssary equipment, weighed no more than 2,200 pounds. Because of the front-end location of the engine, the rear axles carried only about 700 pounds, and the preloading of the wheels to even out cornering placed less weight on the right rear wheel, which ran over Floyd, than on the left. The wide flat-faced treadless tires further reduced the pounds per square inch. Also the car, moving on the jack, probably struck a glancing rather than a maximum blow to Floyd's chest. He had escaped with a momentary loss of wind and minor bruises!

A pit steward sprinted up. "Hurry, Doc," he cried. "I've got trouble over by the gate. It's Phil. He's out cold."

Seeing that Floyd had suffered nothing too serious, Doc left him with his assistant and accompanied the steward to the second victim.

Phil was still unconscious. His improper heartbeat told Doc that more than trackside care was needed. "Get the ambulance over here!" he yelled.

Phil Garrett was to recover without lasting effects. But he was still out cold from shock when the ambulance rolled up.

One of the men who lifted him gently inside was his best friend, Floyd Whitfield — the man whom he had run over and thought he had killed!

Lights Out

The midget racers always drew a big crowd at the Fairbury, Illinois, Motordome. On a September night in 1940, the crowd numbered one too many.

The fans' favorite event at the Motordome was the three-lap Trophy Dash in which four cars, the ones with the fastest times in the lap trials, competed for a winner-take-all cash prize.

The driver with the best time that evening was Wally Zale. Wally led Pete Romcevich, Mike O'Halloran, and Paul Russo on the pace lap that got everyone into proper position for the start.

The four Offenhauser-powered midgets moved faster as they headed down the backstretch. When they clamored out of the turn toward the flagman, they were moving at racing speed. The green flag wig-wagged, and the race began.

The crowd was rising to its feet when it happened. Every light at the track went out!

Mechanics could hear the engines shutting off and imagined the problems the drivers were having in the pitch blackness trying to bring their racers to a safe stop from racing speed. There was a mad scramble to find flashlights, and then a stumbling footrace to the general area of the cars.

Miraculously none of the drivers was injured. One car had spun into the crash wall, but escaped with minor damage. It seemed all was well.

A four-cylinder Offenhauser-powered midget racer. This one, with "slick" tires, is set up for an asphalt track; dirt track racers would use tires with treads.

Push trucks (midget racers carry no starters and must be pushed to start) were arriving with headlights ablaze. The fans settled back and waited for the lights to come on again and the racing to resume.

In a few minutes the lights were restored. As the racers were being pushed down the back stretch, Wally Zale in the lead car began to wave wildly and point ahead.

In the middle of the track lay a man! He was stretched across the racing surface, unconscious.

Where had he come from? He was not with any of the racing crews. He was not a speedway employee. Yet there he was!

The track ambulance was summoned, and the medic was able to revive him. Sheepish and still a little groggy, the stranger cleared up the mystery of his out-of-thin-air appearance.

He was, he confessed, a nonpaying spectator. His seat was a limb high in a tree bordering the rear fence of the track. As the Trophy Dash was his favorite event, he had been hanging far out on the limb to get a better view of the cars as they raced off the turn and passed beneath him.

The cars were entering the turn when he felt his grip give way. He began to fall. The speedway lights went out as he tumbled from the tree to the track below.

What would have happened had the lights stayed on and the race continued?

Would the drivers have been able to stop their speeding midgets? Hardly. They would have tried to swerve to avoid the still form...and hit the fence or each other.

It was by a stroke of luck that the lights went out when they did. Seconds later would have brought death and disaster.

The Unbelievable Boards

Speed!

The urge to go faster has challenged daring men and women in every generation.

Today Indianapolis stands as the royal palace of speed. The annual 500-mile car race attracts a bigger crowd than any other sports event in the world.

Yet the Indianapolis speedway was not always king. At a time when cars were lucky to go faster than 100 mph at Indy, other tracks were yielding speeds of 125 to 135 mph! For example, a speed of over 147 mph was recorded at the Atlantic City, New Jersey, track in 1927. Not until 1960 did any car go that fast at Indianapolis.

What kind of surface allowed such speeds on these tracks? Brick...asphalt...a magical mixture of concrete?

Believe it or not, the answer is wood.

Before Indy was built in 1910, most auto races took place over public roads. Closed circuit races were held on horse tracks. The soft dirt on the roads and tracks was fine for hoofs, but it put spin under tires and dirt in drivers' eyes.

Fred E. Moskovics, an auto engineer, heard about the brick-paved speedway being built at Indianapolis. He believed that an automobile track would also be popular in California.

In his youth Moskovics had watched indoor bike races on wood tracks. Why not an automobile track built of wood? It would be safe, fast, and easier to construct than brick.

At Playa del Rey, a few miles south of Los Angeles, he directed the building of a one-mile board track. The first race, held on April 8, 1910, was a ringing success.

The track itself was something of a wonder. Moskovics called it a "huge wood saucer." Steeply banked and perfectly round, it had wood supports of the type used in bridges. The racing surface, made of two-by-fours laid on edge, was smooth, easy on tires, dust free, and very fast.

Before long, board tracks sprouted up across the country. Crowds grew in size, and promoters looked for greater thrills. Straightaways were introduced, giving cars a chance to run faster and pass more easily. The circular track was replaced by the oval.

This two-mile board track, built near Miami, Florida, was used only once before it was destroyed by a hurricane in September, 1926 (bottom picture).

The constant increase in speeds brought problems to the oval. The corners were simply wrong. Drivers complained that at high speeds they became tricky and dangerous.

Something had to be done. Builders, however, were at a loss to design a track with a smooth even entry from the straightaway into the corners.

All experiments failed. Speeds seemed doomed to the limitations of the tracks. Then Art Pillsbury came up with a solution.

Pillsbury had never designed a board track. But he knew a lot about railroads. He borrowed the basic design of railroad track cornering and used it in building a mile and a quarter speedway at Beverly Hills. Suddenly drivers had no more worries about corners.

The railroad design, known as the Searless Spiral Easement Curve, had been perfected years before to allow the lumbering top-heavy steam engines and freight cars to round a corner without turning over. The SSEC was a series of gradual corners blended together to form a smooth easy approach to any turn.

With the cornering puzzle solved, auto racing was freed to make giant advances. Engine development, oil and fuel improvements, supercharging, streamlining, and strong lightweight alloys all came about during the era of the board tracks.

The Chevrolet Story

Chevrolet is a name we all know today.

Ever wonder where it came from?

We know of Henry Ford. We have heard of Walter P. Chrysler and the Dodge brothers. But unless we read automobile history, we are not likely to find any mention of a hard-luck genius named Louis Chevrolet.

In the early days of automobile development, every American knew of him. Louis Chevrolet was the most famous racing car driver, designer, and builder in the country. The president of General Motors, William Durant, hired him to design and build a passenger car.

In 1912 the first Chevrolet automobile was introduced to the public. It was a large and powerful car of high quality — and an immediate success.

Did Louis Chevrolet become director of Chevrolet Motors? Maybe he just took his money and retired to a beautiful yacht—that is why we haven't heard about him before, right?

Wrong—that would be too simple. Louis Chevrolet's life was never simple.

Once the Chevrolet was accepted as a good automobile, William Durant wanted a few changes. He told Louis to redesign the car...make it less costly. A cheaper Chevrolet would sell by the millions.

Louis refused. He wanted nothing to do with a car of poorer quality. He resigned from the company.

A tragedy! For Durant was right. The less expensive Chevrolet was a smashing success and did sell by the millions.

Was that the end of Louis Chevrolet? No, indeed. The world was to hear more from him—much more.

Louis returned to auto racing. He designed and built a series of very fast cars. They were so fast that they won most of the big races in the country after World War I. Among his victories were the Indianapolis 500-mile races of 1920 and 1921.

Louis was at the peak of his career. Once again he was world famous, the greatest auto engineer of his time, and wealthy. Did he retire now?

Louis Chevrolet at the wheel of his own entry in the Indy 500 of 1920.
Though his car was sidelined by a minor flaw, Louis's brother, Gaston,
won the race in a twin machine.

He did not. Although he could hold onto a steering wheel at high speeds, he could not hold onto his money.

He was hired by the Stutz Motor Car Company to design another new car. It was to be what is called a "sports car." Good looking, fast, and modern in all respects.

Louis designed the finest sports car anyone could imagine. The company officials were excited about his first working model, and it was announced to the world. A factory was opened. Louis, it seemed, was finally going to gain the security of an executive position.

He had designed a fine car; he had done his job well. However, the men who were to raise the money to build the car did not do their jobs well at all. The money was never raised and the factory had to close.

Louis was held responsible for many of the bills. He tried to make good. He drained his wealth trying to pay off the company's debts.

He was down again, but not to stay—not yet. His vast abilities led him into a marvelous new field.

The United States government was looking for up-to-date engines for Army and Navy aircraft. The government asked for engineers to submit designs of small lightweight, yet powerful, engines.

This was all Louis needed to learn. His years of experience in auto racing all had to do with small powerful engines. Moreover he was a pioneer in using aluminum, a lightweight metal, to build them. Louis started work.

As soon as he had his designs on paper, he got financial backing from a friend who ran a Ford dealership. The dealer's name was Glenn L. Martin. They took the designs and working engines to Washington.

The Chevrolet engines were the best submitted and were accepted. Louis could expect a contract as soon as Congress approved the project.

Again fate stepped in. Before he got the approval, there was a nationwide business failure. Government money was needed to support the country. All Army and Navy projects were dropped.

Glenn L. Martin went to California, where he opened an engine manufacturing company. He used the Chevrolet designs as the basis for his production. Today the company is the world leader in aircraft engine manufacture.

Meanwhile, Louis, like many others, was out of work. Jobs were scarce. Few men were working. Louis took what he could. He was hired as a common mechanic by the local Chevrolet garage!

So it was that the brilliant engineer, inventor, and driver was forced to work as a simple repairman on the very cars he had created.

Shortly afterward, Louis suffered a near fatal heart attack and was compelled to retire. In Detroit, home of the Chevrolet Motor Company empire he had helped to found, Louis Chevrolet died penniless.

Bad luck, fate, and unbending idealism had all conspired against him. His only monument—the name of a leading American car.

Two Gallons of Water

The Granatelli brothers, Andy, Joe, and Vince, had purchased a 12-year-old racer. With little money but a lot of know-how, they rebuilt it in their own special way for the 1947 Indianapolis 500-mile race.

Driver Pete Romcevich qualified the car and started 17th in a field of 33. In the opening stages of the race he improved his position steadily. By the 25th lap, he was seventh.

Andy and the crew were elated. Their car, the oldest in the race, was running with the best and sounded great. Who knows, maybe it was their year to win!

Then on the 30th lap they were shaken. Their racer slowed down. Pete pulled into the pits.

Andy ran to see what the trouble was.

"Look down here," Pete said, pointing to the floor of the cockpit.

A glance told Andy they were in deep trouble. The floor-pan of the racer was flooded with engine oil. Somehow their high-powered Ford V8 had developed an oil leak.

Andy was dumbfounded. They had never had any such trouble before. Now all their work and all their dreams were at an end unless he could come up with something.

"Think fast, Andy," he muttered to himself. "Think fast!"

An Indianapolis rule forbids the adding of oil once the race begins. Crews can add fuel, water, and new tires, but no oil.

The rule is meant to safeguard against oil leakage, which can coat the track and cause skidding and accidents.

"I can't add oil,'" Andy mused. "But I can add water!"

As he ran to the hood, he shouted to his brother Joe, "Get me the water can, quick!"

"Did you say the water can?" Joe questioned. He knew the car was not overheating.

Andy shouted back: "Yeah, the water can, and hurry!"

Joe ran to the front of the car as Andy lifted the hood and placed the radiator cap on top, in plain view of the pit inspector who was supervising the work from behind the wall.

As Andy hoisted the water can into position, he quickly pulled off the oil filler cap and dumped two gallons of water into the grumbling engine.

Trying to appear as innocent as possible, he replaced the oil cap, set down the can, and then quickly screwed the radiator cap back in place. As he secured the hood, Joe returned the can to its place.

Pete had been watching from the cockpit with his eyes bugged out. "Water in the oil?" he gasped.

Andy shouted, "Let me hear it, Pete."

The driver hit the throttle. The engine roared.

Andy watched the oil pressure gauge as it struggled upward and leveled off at an acceptable point.

"Get rolling, Pete," he shouted, slapping the astonished driver on the shoulder.

Pete shook his head in disbelief, shifted the racer into gear, and zoomed from the pits.

The Granatelli brothers waited anxiously to see if their racer would make a lap around the track. They did not know what to expect. Then they saw Pete coming down the front straightaway. He *wooshed* by and waved merrily.

The car looked good, sounded good, and every lap brought them closer to the prize money. The

Driver Pete Romcevich at the wheel of # 57 — the Granatelli entry in the 1947 Indy 500 that raced with water as a substitute for lost oil.

brothers hugged each other in their excitement.

Andy used the chalkboard to slow Pete down a bit and to advise him to run as long as the engine would go. Other cars began to drop out. The old car kept going and going. The water had blended with the oil in the engine and allowed the car to continue.

But at the end, it was not the victor. Mauri Rose won the race. The Granatelli car finished 12th.

And it had hung up a track record of sorts. It had run 138 laps—334 miles—with an oil pump pumping water!

The Granatelli brothers took home $2,210.00. Not a bad payment for a moment's quick thinking and two gallons of water.

The Old Warrior

Piero Taruffi was an old man in a young man's world.

His Italian countrymen loved him. In the past they had cheered the triumphs of the "old warrior." Now they wanted him to retire. His hair was white. His strong body was showing age.

For more than 30 years he had driven racing cars. His career glittered with wins, and yet he would have swapped them all for one victory in the Mille Miglia.

The Mille Miglia was the supreme test of road racing. It was 1,000 miles of twistings and turnings through the plains and mountains of Italy.

Since his youth, Taruffi had believed the Mille

Miglia was *his* race. Wasn't it run over countryside he knew like the palm of his hand? Each year he believed that he would win. As a beginner in 1933, he had easily placed third. He had never come close again.

In 1957 the old warrior decided to try once more.

The famed Ferrari factory had entered four cars. Three were to be driven by young champions: Peter Collins of England; Wolfgang Von Trips of Germany; and the Marquis de Portago, a Spanish nobleman.

Taruffi was assigned the fourth car. The choice of the old warrior, the public felt, was a just if emotional reward for his years in the sport.

The four Ferarris had unlimited V12 engines, but the Mille Miglia was open to all cars, large and small. It was a race against time. The small cars started first, 30 seconds apart. The medium and large cars went off later at one minute intervals.

Taruffi arrived in the garage area hours before his starting time. He watched closely as the mechanics made their final check of his blood-red racer. He longed to get going.

The signal finally came. The Ferarri drivers slid into the seats, adjusted their safety harnesses, and started their engines. Amid cries of good luck, they moved to the starting line.

One by one they were checked in, their time

cards marked, and sent roaring southward along the seaside roads of the Adriatic shore. The foursome quickly took over the front positions. Von Trips led, with Collins, Taruffi, and de Portago following in that order.

The narrow, twisting roads suited the style of the English champion, Collins. He overtook Von Trips. Taruffi held onto third, just ahead of de Portago, as they tore through the countryside.

The cars reached the lower part of Italy. From there the course wound westward and then north into the mountains. At each stop, mechanics made emergency repairs, changed spark plugs, and refilled fuel tanks.

It became a test of endurance and grit. Spectators lining the roads saw the toll in dented fenders, scratched paint, and dangling headlights. A lowslung Triumph plunged off the road, killing its driver. The race went on.

By the halfway checkpoint, Collins had stretched his lead to five minutes. Taruffi, using his long experience with the course, had cut the gap between his car and Von Trips's. Starting three minutes behind, he now trailed by only a minute.

The cars climbed into the dangerous mountain circuit, where Taruffi was at home. He drove daringly along the winding switchback sections, brushing the fragile rail guards that fenced high cliffs. He made up time in every turn and took over second place from Von Trips.

The old warrior was driving his greatest race, but so was the Englishman. Collins had opened his lead to eight minutes, and his car was running beautifully.

Out of the mountains and northward they raced. The Ferarris still dominated. With a mere 150 miles to go, they reached the final stop. Collins had built up a mighty 11-minute lead over Taruffi. His car serviced, he dashed away toward seeming victory.

The remainder of the route curved across the top of Italy and toward the finish line in Brescia, the city where the race had begun. Collins forced his car to its limit, intent upon a record. He was still 130 miles short of the goal when the Ferarri coasted to a stop. The drive shaft had broken.

As Collins sat downcast in his seat, Taruffi and Von Trips flashed past. Their battle was no longer for second place. At stake was the lead.

Ten miles farther on, Von Trips edged past the tiring old man. The German, with his three-minute headstart, had to make up those 180 seconds in the final 120 miles.

The final checkpoint showed Taruffi still clinging desperately to a slim time lead. Von Trips was gaining, and so was the fourth member of the Ferarri team, de Portago. Indeed de Portago was gaining on both!

Forty miles to go...the fastest portion of the course. All three Ferarris were running well over 150 mph as they sprinted for the finish.

Just as it appeared that de Portago might overtake Taruffi and Von Trips, his steering mechanism failed. His racer careened into a crowd of spectators. De Portago and his mechanic were killed. Ten spectators died.

News of the tragedy had not yet reached the crowds near Brescia, and they rooted at the top of their lungs for the two leaders sweeping by. Von Trips was in front. Taruffi, close behind, was winning the race on elapsed time. Inside the blood-red racer, however, the old warrior was waging a private battle just to keep going.

His hands on the steering wheel were stiff and numb. His legs knotted with painful cramps. Now and again his vision blurred. Cramped, tortured, and giddy, he forced himself on by desire alone.

He saw the roofs of Brescia rushing closer, and now he was roaring into the city, a journey through streets and through agony. Ahead was the finish line, street banners and bright signs and shouting faces....

Somehow he stopped in the village square. He

slumped forward in the torrid cockpit, exhausted, then he straightened slightly to greet his crew and the swarms of well-wishers.

He had broken the jinx. He had won *his* race!

He took the towering silver trophy home and fell into bed. Deep inside, he knew that if he had lost again, he would have returned next year.

He did not know that another Mille Miglia was not to be. Government officials announced the race would never be held again. It was too dangerous.

After 30 years of heartbreak, Piero Taruffi, the old warrior, had won on his last chance.

The Last Wish

No man ever loved auto racing more than Terrence A. Donnally. It was part of his life, and in death he became part of it too.

He was not a driver though he tried hard to become one. More than heart and desire were needed to make the grade, he learned. His place was in the garage. There he had the touch—as a machinist, welder, metal worker, and engine builder.

When the space center opened at Cape Canaveral, Florida, he saw a larger challenge. He went to work at the rocket base, but he never forgot his first love — auto racing. He and his wife, Reta, spent their weekends at one of the many tracks in the area.

Summer vacations were planned so that they could attend the 600-mile race at the Charlotte Motor Speedway in North Carolina. They watched all the practice sessions and became friends with drivers and mechanics.

The years were bright and full for Terry Donally. Although it had been hard to give up his ambition of driving, he had turned his love of racing into an enriching hobby. He was happily married. He enjoyed his work at the Cape.

Then he began suffering headaches.

At first a simple aspirin chased away the pain. Then the headaches grew worse. His doctor advised a complete examination at the hospital.

Terry piled auto racing magazines on the back seat of his car and drove himself to the hospital. On the way he tried to calm Reta's fears.

"It's going to be great to loll around and catch up on my reading," he said.

After X-rays were taken, Reta was given the crushing news.

"It's a brain tumor," the doctor told her.

An operation was performed. Terry failed to rally.

He called Reta to his bedside. "I have a last wish," he said, and told her exactly what to do.

A telephone call was made to an old friend in Charlotte, Henry Tillman. A second call to Charlotte, this one to another friend, Ralph Moody, chief of the Ford racing team, ironed out the last details.

A few days later, Terry Donnally died at 53.

Reta had the body cremated, as Terry had instructed. She and some friends took the ashes to the Charlotte Motor Speedway, Terry's favorite track. Tillman and Moody were waiting in the pit area.

"I don't know exactly how you want to proceed," Tillman said to Reta. "Ralph and I thought we might drive around the track and spread them..."

"This is good," replied Reta, nodding. "This is good."

She, Tillman, and Moody, along with two close friends, Roger Stovall and Mrs. Dorothy Asendorf, stood in a tight little circle. They bowed their heads as Mrs. Asendorf read out loud from the Bible.

"The Lord is my shepherd..."

Then Tillman, Moody, and Guy Charles, the Speedway office manager, climbed into Moody's car. Tillman held the oblong box Reta had given him. He removed the brown wrapping paper and broke the wax seal.

The car moved onto the track.

Tillman cast the ashes onto the rain-puddled gray asphalt. They drove one lap. The last puff of ashes floated down in front of the grandstand.

Terry Donnally's last wish was fulfilled.

Black Magic Victory

Before he was 30, Eddie Rickenbacker had gained international fame; first as a racing car driver, then as America's leading fighter pilot in World War I.

Later he saved the Indianapolis Speedway from being torn down, and nursed an infant Eastern Airlines into one of the nation's major carriers. Before he died in 1973, he had been an adviser to presidents.

All in all, one can hardly imagine a less likely believer in black magic.

And yet there was that incident in 1913....

Eddie was managing the three-car Duesenberg racing team. Coming into the 300-mile race in

Sioux City, Iowa, the season had been a disaster. The cars hadn't won a thing.

A meager seven dollars was left in the racing fund. It was not enough to rent proper facilities; the cars had to be parked under the grandstand. The seven crew members had to sleep in a single room.

Eddie's mother lived nearby, and he unburdened his woes to her one evening over dinner. She listened patiently. Then she suggested a remedy from the folklore of her native Switzerland.

She told him to catch a bat, cut out the heart, and tie it to his middle finger with a red silk thread. The charm would insure success.

Eddie knew she meant well. So he thanked her gratefully while he winced inwardly.

In the early trial runs, the Duesenbergs were far from the fastest cars. Moreover the tire and mechanical problems that had plagued them in previous races left doubts as to how long they would last.

Eddie was discouraged. On the outcome of this one race depended the future of the Duesenberg racing effort. It was win or disband.

He watched the other cars run and tried to develop a plan for victory. It seemed the only chance was a longshot: Run at full throttle from the start and hope the engines held together and the tires did not blow.

Throughout the week of preparation, his mother's words haunted him. He knew they were nonsense. Still he could not stop thinking about a bat's heart and a red silk thread.

"Why not?" he found himself thinking as race day drew near. "We've tried everything else without success. What can we lose?"

He told a local farm boy that he would pay a silver dollar for a live bat. The night before the race, the boy delivered it.

Eddie carried it into a shed the next morning. The heart was removed and tied carefully to his middle finger with red silk thread. Quickly pulling on his racing gloves, he strode toward the racer.

He was ready for anything.

The race was fast and wild. Cars crashed. Others were forced out by the pace. A car driven by J.W. Cox nicked Eddie's front wheel, rolled over, and killed both Cox and his riding mechanic.

Eddie's car held up. He was battling for the lead as the final five laps were signaled. Suddenly a large rock, thrown up by the wheels of another racer, struck his mechanic in the forehead.

The man was knocked unconscious and sagged in his seat. Eddie had to take over his duties of maintaining the oil and fuel pressure while driving at top speed.

During the final laps, Eddie ran in a duel with Spencer Wisehart. Wisehart's Mercer was faster down the long straightaways. Eddie managed the turns quicker. They traded the front position time and again.

In a superb finish, Eddie forged off the final turn and hung on grimly. The faster Wisehart couldn't catch him before the checkered flag fell.

Eddie had won, and a teammate, Tom Alley, finished third. The team's winnings amounted to $12,500. Duesenberg's racing future was secure.

Success had resulted from a combination of smart tactics and plain hard driving. But hard driving had caused engine and tire failure in the past. Why did those balky engines run so well? What kept the tires from bursting again? Was

Eddie Rickenbacker's Duesenberg in the Indianapolis Speedway Museum.

some mysterious force guarding the luck of Eddie Rickenbacker and his team that day in Iowa?

Afterward, whenever he was asked about the race, Eddie smiled a funny smile.

"Sometimes," he answered, "things happen to make you wonder."

The Hard-Way Champion

Racing fans in Florida knew Alan "Rags" Carter as the driver who never quit trying.

On the night of January 16, 1952, Rags drove a typical all-out race, and his will to win hurtled him into the weirdest finish of all time.

The race was for the Florida Stock Car Championship — 50 laps around the Opa Locka Speedway. Thirty-four drivers, the high point winners on a night-to-night basis during the season, lined up two abreast. The fewer points a driver won, the nearer the front he started. Rags started in the very last row.

As he pulled his Guthrie Auto Repair Dodge #3 into position, he waved to the driver beside him,

Edwin "Banjo" Matthews. Banjo, seated in his H.C. Wilcox Ford #28, waved back.

Before the race was over, they would see a lot of each other. Banjo's driving style was dogged and rough, for which the grandstand regulars had dubbed him "The Opa Locka Wild Man." In his own way, he tried as hard as Rags. Each respected the other.

The drivers were motioned ahead, and they traveled slowly around the oval. As they passed the starter's stand, they watched for the signal to go ahead, switch positions, or do whatever was needed to get all machines in proper order for a start the next time around.

The pace increased as the field rolled down the backstretch. The drivers in front wanted to get the jump on the faster entries behind them and take an early lead. They were racing when they swept off the turn and headed toward Bob Verlin, high above the track in the starter's stand.

Verlin, holding both a yellow and a green flag, watched the field closely. If the cars were in good order, he would drop the green and send them on their way. If not, the yellow would be waved to signal one more lap around.

Things looked good to Verlin, and he shouted, "Let's go!" Jumping high, he whipped the green flag.

Smoke from roaring engine exhausts and spinning tires filled the air. Rags and Banjo accelerated with the group.

Trouble often develops on the first few laps when traffic is thickest, and it happened that night.

Two cars locked bumpers ahead of Banjo and jammed his line. Experience had taught him to look far ahead, and he was quick to take advantage. He whipped #28 to the left and bolted onto the inner edge of the track. It was bumpy but clear. He gained 10 positions on Rags, who was stymied in the rear.

As the race progressed, the field thinned out and the faster cars fought their way toward the front. The halfway mark found Banjo leading. Rags and his #3 Dodge were far back, mired by heavy traffic near the middle of the field. He had been bottled up since the start and was unable to use all his horsepower.

As Rags came down the backstretch, an opening finally appeared. He toed the throttle, and the Dodge responded with a burst of speed. Needling through the gap, he passed two cars before he reached the turn. He handled the car expertly and hit the frontstretch with his throttle on the floor. It was his first chance to run, and he had ground to make up.

The #3 Dodge gave the fans their money's worth in the next few laps. Driving like a demon,

Rags was passing cars on the outside and inside, sometimes two cars at a time.

The front-running Banjo, however, wasn't easing up. He could see the Dodge in his rearview mirror and was driving wide open to hold his lead.

Coming out of the turn and down the front-stretch, Banjo saw Bob Verlin leaning over the track. The starter held five fingers up. That meant five laps to go — a bit more than 100 seconds of racing left. Could he hold off Rags? Confidently he shoved his foot down on the throttle even harder.

But in the next lap he suddenly had company.

The #3 Dodge was tight against his bumper. Banjo felt a sharp nudge from his challenger. He had expected it; he had handled the rough stuff before. It was part of stock car racing.

Out of the turn and down the backstretch they raced, the #3 Dodge locked against the leader's bumper. Into the next turn, a good nudge, but no change in positions. Banjo was still in command.

Rags realized there was only one way to win — use the outside lane to pass. The going is always tough out there: The track is slippery and the distance farther around. Then too there is the crash wall. A slight slip and *pfft*! A wrecked car, no prize money, and the possibility of an injury. Should he try it, or settle for a safe and certain second place?

Rags Carter was not a man to settle for second if there was a chance to win. He decided instantly.

As the cars leaped off the turn, he veered into the dangerous outside lane.

Rags buzzed the crash wall as they sped up the frontstretch and wheeled in beside Banjo. They stayed even, neither able to gain the lead. Side by side they ran, a perfect match of skill and speed.

Every fan was standing as the drivers fought wheel to wheel through the last laps. Here was racing at its best!

The white flag waved. The last lap! Still Rags and Banjo remained side by side — through the turn, down the backstretch, and into the final turn.

As they battled through the corner and out for the run to the finish line, Rags saw his chance. A slower yellow car was riding the inner edge of the track. If he could keep Banjo behind the yellow car, the race was his. He held his #3 Dodge tight against Banjo's right side.

Bob Verlin, raising the checkered flag, saw what Rags was doing. The fans saw it. Banjo saw it. Rags was pulling the oldest maneuver in auto racing, using the slower traffic to block off an opponent.

Banjo reacted quickly to avoid the trap. He tried to steer around the blocking car. But Rags was pressing against his door, using all his skill to hold Banjo's #28 where it was. The two cars were jammed together — doors, side bars, fenders, and tires — rubbing and bumping as they headed for the finish line.

The last 75 yards was the race. The previous laps meant nothing.

Rags was being thrust outward toward the crash wall. Centrifugal force was carrying his #3 Dodge far to the outside. Was there room between the yellow car and the wall?

Rags saw the finish line just ahead and the mass of the wall beside him. He was too near...too near....

Banjo, meanwhile, fought his car outward. He had to get by the yellow car or crash into its rear. It was too late to slow down; he had to go through with his attempt to squeeze between Rags and the yellow car. He held his throttle foot down and gripped the steering wheel tighter.

In a flash he was through. He nicked the rear corner of the yellow car, but got by. Now the finish line...just before him. The two leaders raced for it, still locked side by side.

Suddenly the fans screamed in fright.

The outside rear wheel of Rags's Dodge caught the crash wall. The Dodge twisted, crashing into Banjo's Ford and causing it to spin across the track and onto the infield grass.

Rags's Dodge, completely out of control, smashed the wall again and rammed its right front wheel. The car shot high into the air, a gyrating mass of metal. As it went up, the wheels stuck fast in the fence and wrenched the front axles from its mounts.

The racer flew through the air, turning over and around before crashing back onto the track. Landing on its steel top, it skidded wildly amid a shower of sparks as the metal ground away on the hot pavement. Inside, Rags held on for his life.

The sturdy roll bars and safety belt saved him. When all the cars had stopped, he struggled from the overturned racer.

The track photographer rushed over and snapped the picture. It was featured in newspapers from coast to coast, accompanied by a story of the Florida championship race.

Yes, Rags had won. He had crossed the finish line without a front axle or wheels, skidding upside down and backwards!

Birth of a Racing Car

It was 1910, and the light-car race near Paris, France, had concluded four hours ago. Now three of the drivers sat in a cafe, sipping wine and grumbling bitterly.

The Italian, Paolo Zucarrelli, had seemingly little reason to complain. He had won the race in his Spanish-built Hispano Suiza. The other two, Jules Goux and Georges Boillot, were Frenchmen who drove for the Peugeot Company of France. All three were top-ranked drivers in the light-car class.

And yet they were discontented and frustrated. Each had ambitions of moving up to the unlimited class where the fastest cars raced and the rewards were greatest. Unfortunately, openings for drivers of unlimited cars were scarce.

The talk went round and round the subjects of racing — owners, cars, designers — till all at once Goux banged a fist on the table.

"Who knows better than a driver what is needed to win races?" he demanded angrily.

"We could design a faster car than any textbook engineer," asserted Boillot confidently. "I know we could!"

Goux called for pencils and paper as glasses and ashtrays were pushed aside. In the flickering candlelight the first tentative outline of a new kind of racing machine took shape.

Getting down all their ideas took many days. The process of getting the products of three minds to mesh was often a trial of patience. But at last rough sketches were completed. The threesome felt certain they had conceived the ideal Grand Prix racer.

What they required next were a shop and money. Goux was appointed to speak with the owner of the Peugeot Company and seek his help.

Robert Peugeot studied the sketches Goux laid on his desk. He was impressed.

"I'll back you," he announced. "We have a small shop just outside Paris that you may use."

The rough sketches had to be redrawn before construction could begin. A draftsman, Ernest

Henry, was hired for the job. Henry was not an engineer, but he had the gift of grasping an idea and putting it on paper.

When the news leaked out that three drivers and a draftsman had teamed up, the small shop became the butt of jokes. Three drivers design a car? It made no more sense than letting a jockey operate on a horse.

The French automotive industry had its laugh. Then it forgot about the small shop and the starry-eyed drivers.

In 1912 it got a jolting reminder.

The Peugeot was introduced to competition in no less an event than the Grand Prix of France. This was the greatest race of the year, an open contest of 950 miles that drew the best cars in Europe. Georges Boillot was chosen to drive.

Ignored at the start, the Peugeot, when it crossed the finish line, was the center of all eyes. No wonder. It was all alone. Cornering and climbing like a jackrabbit, the car simply ran away from the field.

The racing world was stunned. The Fiat team had previously held total mastery over European road races. Their huge all-conquering cars, with engines two and a half times that of the Peugeot's, had performed as well as ever. Yet the nimble brainchild of three drivers had left them wallowing behind.

Jules Goux in the Peugeot that won the 1913 Indy 500. Designed by Goux and two friends in 1910, the Peugeot is still the basis for all ultra-high racing engines to this day.

Sparked by success, the small shop built more cars, each an improvement over the last. The cars entered hill climbs, reliability tests, and straight speed runs. The type of race mattered little. The Peugeots were seldom beaten.

By 1913 there were 10 Peugeots spinning dust and mud over the competition. Their fame spread to America. A letter arrived inviting the Peugeots to enter the Indianapolis 500.

Goux and Zucarrelli crossed the Atlantic with two of the older models. The drivers had heard that American racing was much like a cowboy show: rough, dirty, and little money. They went for fun, and they didn't want to bust up their best cars.

77

Upon reaching Indianapolis, they realized their mistake. The track was excellent, the organization tight, and the prize money large. They decided to go all out.

A few trial runs convinced them that their tires were inadequate for the harsh brick surface. They switched to American tires and hired an American driver, Johnny Aitken, to coach them.

The Peugeots had the speed, Aitken saw immediately. His main concern was teaching the foreigners to maintain a proper pace — fast enough to win, but not so fast as to wear out the tires before the finish.

Aitken got his lessons across. Zucarrelli fared poorly, being forced out on the 18th lap with main-bearing failure. But Goux won, coasting to a record-breaking victory 13 minutes ahead of the second-place finisher!

The Indianapolis victory established the Peugot as a supercar. Overnight the racing world began copying it. The three drivers and a draftsman, toiling without even a consulting engineer, had wrought a small miracle.

Today, more than half a century later, the Peugeot design is still the basis for all ultra-high horsepower racing engines. All unlimited-Grand-Prix, racing boat, and Indianapolis engines trace their ancestry to the discontent of three drivers that evening in 1910.

The Voices of Harry Miller

The streets of Menomonie, a lumber town in Wisconsin, resounded with fierce noises. People tumbled out of bed and rushed to the windows.

What they beheld was mind-boggling. Harry Miller, 24, was riding his bicycle.

Only Miller wasn't peddling!

The furious sputters and backfiring came from a small one-cylinder engine mounted on the bike. It was the year 1899 and zipping down the street was the first motorcycle ever built in America.

The gasping townsfolk were astonished by the motorcycle, not by Miller. A hometown boy, he had a reputation for tinkering and inventing. Some people even whispered that he heard voices... voices telling him what to build and how.

The voices — if they were voices — apparently inspired Miller just so far. He never bothered to refine or patent his early inventions. Once he had proved they worked, he lost interest.

The little engine on his bike was useful. It got him to his job. That was enough. He never earned a nickel from it although it was the forerunner of the motorcycle industry.

In the summer of 1899 he built another engine, a small four-cylinder unit. Clamping it to the stern of his rowboat, he putt-putted around a fishing lake near Menomonie.

When winter came, he moved to California. He took his bride, but not his motorized rowboat. He simply forgot about it.

Someone else did not. A machinist friend took it home and studied the design. The next year, 1900, he put on the market a two-cylinder model and eventually became a multimillionaire. The man was Olie Evinrude, called "the father of the outboard engine." Today Evinrude is among the biggest names in outboard motors.

Miller settled in Los Angeles. The automobile fascinated him, and he built one for himself. Soon he developed a revolutionary carburetor.

Called "The Master," the carburetor sold more than 5,000 units a month for years. This time

Harry Miller protected himself by obtaining patents, and he became rich.

Money alone did not satisfy him. Restlessly he groped and strove — and acted strangely.

"I have... supernatural powers," he admitted.

He could take complete sentences from a person's mouth before they were spoken. He predicted deaths though often he had never seen the subject except in a photograph.

While wrestling with a problem he would sit trancelike for hours preparing his mind for his voices. Then he would work for days without rest.

Was Harry Miller a genius? Or were the mysterious voices — "control" he called them — responsible for all his ideas?

Whichever it was, he continued to bring forth a bounty of inventions.

He developed a novel spark plug. The patent was purchased by the Peerless Motor Car Company.

He perfected the first successful aluminum piston, which he produced and sold by the thousands.

He pioneered lightweight aluminum aircraft engines. The government paid him $50,000 to head the development of a large engine. He quit when he was offered a chance to work on fuel-pump and carburetor research with a small automobile firm.

The automobile had become his passion, and success brought him to the attention of the people in racing. They began coming to him for answers to their problems. He opened his own shop, and the top names in the sport became his steady customers.

In 1916 the renowned driver Barney Oldfield gave him a contract for $15,000 — a staggering sum in that day — to build a racer. The next year Miller delivered the "Golden Submarine," the first fully enclosed and streamlined speedway racer. Oldfield drove it to a string of victories and world records.

The "voices" seemed to be directing Miller at a fever pitch now. His name went into the record books for both speedboats and racing cars. From 1922, the year of his first victory at Indianapolis, until well into the 1930's, Miller entries won more than 80 percent of the 500-mile races!

Then in the 1930's he faltered. Friends close to him hinted that he had lost his "control."

Henry Ford didn't think so. The automobile maker hired Miller to design 10 Indianapolis racers, using Ford V8 engines and other stock parts.

In the trials they were the fastest entries along the straightaways and seemed sure winners. But in the race itself, they dropped out one by one.

Miller had placed the exhaust pipe too near the steering unit. As the race wore on, the heat caused the grease in the steering to melt. Without lubrication, the steering locked. The man who was famed

Henry Miller — a dapper eccentric genuis. He invented the first "motorcycle," and the first "motorboat." In 1935 he designed ten racing cars for the Ford Motor Co. They used souped-up 1935 Ford V8 engines and a 1935 Ford grill as nosepieces. Ted Horn drove # 43.

for his attention to detail had made a colossal blunder.

It was the time of the Great Depression, and Miller had to close his plant. He traveled to Detroit to find work.

The auto companies needed educated, conservative engineers. Miller was a bold inventor and innovator who had quit school at 13. He couldn't find a job.

His health failed. Surgery did not arrest the cancer in his cheek. Despondent, he moved to a shabby room in Detroit's tenement district.

He lived alone and hid from the world. Disfigured by pain and disease, he refused to allow even his wife to stay with him. His only visitor was Edward Offult, a former employee. During Miller's last days, they worked together on the design of a new automobile.

On May 3, 1943, Harry Miller died, alone.

He had, perhaps, foreseen his own death as he had foreseen the deaths of many others and did not wish to be a burden.

And the voices?

They had not deserted him after all.

Among the cheap furniture in his room stood his drawing board. On it was the design of a small, front-drive car with automatic transmission.

It was 10 years ahead of its time.

A Glance Upward — and Backward

Ray Harroun had just completed the qualifying run for the first 500-mile race at Indianapolis in 1911.

His Marmon Wasp had roared down the quarter-mile strip of straightaway at better than the required speed of 75 mph. Harroun seemed assured of a starting place.

His crew was still congratulating him when the track's chief judge walked into the garage.

"I'm sorry to tell you this, Ray," he said. "It looks like your car will be disqualified."

"Are you kidding?" gasped Harroun.

"No, I'm not," the judge replied. "The other drivers are protesting. They claim your car is hazardous. You have no riding mechanic. There's no one to tell you when a car is coming up behind you to pass."

The Marmon Wasp was the only single-seater in the race. All the other cars had a riding mechanic seated beside the driver.

"The race is only two days off!" bellowed Harroun. "I don't have time to rebuild my car to carry a mechanic!"

"It may be too late to change the car, but it's not too late to accept the drivers' protest," said the judge. "I'm sorry, Ray."

"Ridiculous...absolutely ridiculous!" grumbled the outraged Harroun.

The judge returned to the track, where further time trials were being run. Harroun left the garage muttering in disgust.

The mechanics shifted their attention to the other Marmon entry, a two-seater. They talked about Harroun being used as a relief driver in the bigger car. The single-seater, it seemed, was out of the race.

Or was it?

Later that day, Harroun entered the garage and began to work by himself. He took out a welding torch and metal saw and got busy.

Soon he had completed a sturdy frame for a little mirror he had purchased in town. The mirror was eight inches long and three inches wide.

Harroun mounted it five inches above the front

edge of the cowling. This was high enough for him to see under it without ducking his head. A quick glance upward gave him a clear view of a car approaching from the rear. The sturdy frame kept down vibrations.

The judges had never seen anything quite like it. But they decided it was as good as an assistant to warn Harroun of cars overtaking him. The protests of the drivers were overruled. The Marmon Wasp was in the lineup on the morning of May 30, 1911.

Few thought Harroun could compete without a mechanic. His little mirror was the object of endless jests. He didn't care. Once on the track, he showed how well the little mirror replaced the extra weight of a mechanic. As the miles passed, Harroun's single-seater Marmon Wasp gained on the leader. After 150 miles, it was running second.

The lead changed hands a number of times. Then with 19 laps to go, Harroun spurted to the front and stayed there.

He beat the second place car by a full lap!

Ray Harroun accomplished far more than winning a race, however. He had invented and proved the usefulness of one of the most important safety devices the modern motorist has on his car today — the rearview mirror.

The little piece of glass stuck on the cowling of Harroun's car was soon adapted to passenger cars

A close-up view of the very first rear-view mirror, and an action shot of the inventor, Ray Harroun, and his car, the Marmon Wasp.

and trucks. From this idea developed the side mirror. Today the driver on the highway can gauge his distance from the car behind, as well as the car in front, while traveling at high speeds. The mirrors tell him when the car behind is about to pass him, and how much time he must allow to slow down in order to avoid a collision from the rear.

So Harroun's determination to drive alone and save the weight of the mechanic has also prevented countless highway accidents and saved hundreds of lives. A good example of how car racing often benefits the motorist in his everyday driving.

Marge vs. the St. Louis Cardinals

The St. Louis Cardinals, World Series Champions of 1934, never forgave Marge Russo.

Marge didn't play baseball. She was a racing car driver from a racing family. Her older brother, Joe, was a veteran of Indianapolis. Her younger brother, Paul, and her uncle, Eddie, would drive at Indy too.

Marge was an exhibition driver who also took on men in match races throughout the Midwest. One of her tricks was to drive an open cockpit racer around the track at top speed—*blindfolded.*

In 1934 the Chicago midget racing season opened with night competition at Kostner Stadium. Marge was featured in a match race against a former Indianapolis winner, Louis Schneider. Little did she foresee that a switch in her opponent would cause a furor in the sports world.

The Chicago Cubs baseball team played a game against the St. Louis Cardinals on the afternoon of the midget races. Johnny O'Hara, radio announcer of the Cubs games, was also track announcer at the midget auto races. After the Cubs-Cardinal game, he invited three of the Cardinal stars to go to the races with him. The players were Dizzy Dean, his brother Daffy, both pitchers, and the fiery third baseman Pepper Martin.

At the speedway the ballplayers were introduced to the opening night crowd and received a standing ovation. As the players watched the races, track manager Al Sweeney mentioned that Marge was to run against Schneider later in the evening.

The fun-loving Dizzy Dean urged Sweeney to change the match race. Instead of Schneider, let Pepper Martin drive against her! Martin owned and drove race cars in Oklahoma. Dizzy and Daffy had seen him drive.

Sweeney grabbed at the match-up. The publicity would be tremendous. He announced the news to the crowd.

Martin could handle a bat and glove, but could he handle a powerful midget race car? The excited fans soon found out.

The two cars were brought to the starting line, and Marge and Pepper got into the snug-fitting cockpits. They took a few warm-up laps and then fell into position side by side. The race was on.

It was immediately obvious that Martin could handle the car. He got into a tense, wheel-to-wheel duel with his female opponent. They ran evenly until the fourth lap, when the engine in Marge's racer quit. She pulled to the side.

Martin's racer was running flawlessly. Being a showman, he continued to roar around the track. He thrilled the fans as he threw dirt sky-high with his broadsliding antics in each turn. The fans cheered him on to faster speeds.

All at once Martin lost control of the car. It spun violently and crashed into the outside retaining wall.

Everyone at the speedway was horrified. Here was Pepper Martin, one of the biggest names in baseball, jammed against the crash wall in a smoking broken race car. Was he hurt?

Luckily Martin was only stunned. He and the Dean brothers were hustled to the railroad station in time to make the trip back to St. Louis with the rest of the team.

Sweeney, meanwhile, telephoned the story to the Chicago newspapers. It was put on the coast-to-coast wire service. The next day newspapers from New York to Los Angeles carried the report of the Russo-Martin race and its nearly disastrous climax.

"Pepper Martin Escapes Death in Racing

Crash." Cardinal manager Frankie Frisch saw the headline and hit the ceiling. He called the three players into his office.

Was it true? Had they been at the speedway? Did Martin risk his high-priced neck in such a scatterbrained stunt?

"The three guys at the speedway must have been imposters," insisted the glib Dizzy Dean. He hoped Sweeney would cover for them. "Check it out."

Frisch called the track manager. From the anger in Frisch's voice, Sweeney realized the players were in hot water. To rescue them, he replied that the story was a hoax. He blamed his overzealous publicity man for dreaming it up.

Everyone involved breathed a sigh of relief. Everyone but manager Frisch.

He rewrote the contracts of all the players in the Cardinal organization. When the next season rolled around, the players were forbidden to own a race car, to drive a race car, and even to work on a race car.

The unwitting cause of all the fuss was little Marge Russo, who continued to thrill racetrack crowds.

The St. Louis players, however, never appreciated her talents.

"She should have stayed in the kitchen," snorted Pepper Martin.

The Warnings

Dick Losenbeck was 32 when he died. A hard-working practical man, he made his own way. He had no use for superstitions that so often sway racing drivers.

Had he believed in omens just a mite, Dick Losenbeck might be alive today.

Dick operated Fleet Lubrication, Inc., a firm that maintained trucks belonging to other companies in Miami, Florida. He loved his work, his family, and his hobby of driving racing stock cars.

Recently he had bought a powerful V8 machine to run in the modified class. It replaced his old six-cylinder stocker. To gain experience with the faster car, he raced it every chance he got.

On Friday afternoon, April 27, 1973, Dick should have been loading up to drive to the Palm Beach Speedway in West Palm Beach, Florida. Instead he was heading for a nearby hospital. His older son, Mike, 11, was recovering from an appendectomy. Dick had decided to forego the race that night.

He was chatting at his son's bedside. After a few minutes, Mike said, "Heck, Dad. I'm doing great. You go on."

Dick considered whether he could still make the 75-mile trip. Was there time? He telephoned his mechanic from the hospital.

The mechanic didn't like the idea. He pointed out that to arrive late at a race was asking for trouble. The engine must be made to run perfectly. The car must be tested for handling. The driver must warm up and get the feel of things.

"There won't be enough time tonight," the mechanic protested. Dick overruled him. He had made up his mind to run.

The two men met at the garage and discovered that the race trailer had a flat tire. The mechanic saw the flat as another reason for not going. Dick viewed it as only an annoying delay.

"Let's forget it," said the mechanic.

Dick overruled him again. The tire was changed, and they drove to the speedway.

After the car was fueled, Dick got in and took a

few slow laps. With the engine warmed up, he got on the throttle. The car raced into the turn.

Suddenly it slid sideways toward the crash wall. Dick whipped the wheel to the right, relaxed on the throttle a hair, and powered the car through. He returned at once to the pits.

"I thought you had yourself a piece of the wall, Dick," said his worried mechanic.

"She sure isn't handling," Dick said. He was undecided. "What do you think?"

"It's the track," said the mechanic. "Rain has washed all the rubber out. It's slick as glass. Let's go home and get her set up for the Hialeah Speedway tomorrow night."

Dick thought a moment, running his hand through his thinning brown hair. He wanted the practice in the car.

"We probably should quit now," he said. "But let's work on it a bit. I'll line up at the rear of my races and see how she goes."

He was scheduled in the second heat, and he took a position at the tail. The field moved off as the green flag waved. Dick played it carefully.

He made no attempt to race with the others. Nevertheless he passed another straggler, Don Christie. Christie, a good friend, was running poorly and fell farther and farther behind.

During the first few laps, Dick felt his car out. It

was performing better. Encouraged, he gunned it down the straightway, through the first and second turns, and built up speed again on the backstretch.

As he started to accelerate in the fourth turn, the rear wheels seemed to lose traction. The car looped into the infield. Keeping the power on, he corrected for the spin in an effort to get back into the race.

The tactics were wrong. The car spun again, and stalled. It ended sitting crosswise on the track.

Dick reached forward to start the engine. He could see Christie running through the turn behind him. The engine refused to start. Had Christie seen him?

Christie hadn't. He came on.

The crowd waited for the evasive action. It never occurred. At the last instant, Christie locked his brakes, but his car slammed into Dick's at the driver's door. The brightly colored racers banged along the track, eventually halting in front of the main grandstand.

Warning lights flashed. The race stopped. Emergency crews rushed to the crash. Christie jumped from his car unhurt. There was no movement from the other car.

The rescue squad used a torch to cut through the metal and free Dick. He was lifted unconscious from the track by a helicopter and flown to a hospital. His skull was fractured, and he died the next day.

"It seems like fate was trying all day to tell Dick not to race," his mechanic remarked. "Time and again we nearly packed it, but we didn't. Man, I wish we had listened."

Would You Believe?

First U.S. Automobile Race

The first auto race in the United States was held in Illinois on Thanksgiving Day, 1895.

The route was the round trip between downtown Chicago and Evanston. The field consisted of six entries; four powered by gasoline and two by electricity.

Two cars finished the run through the freezing cold, over roads piled high with slush. The winner, Frank Duryea, drove a gasoline-powered auto of his own design, beating an imported Benz.

Time for the 54-mile run was 10 hours and 33 minutes, an average speed of 5.1186 mph.

What the Flags Mean

In auto racing, flags are used to advise the drivers of the progress of the race or to give them orders. Each flag has a different color and meaning.

Green: Start the race. Continue the race—the course is clear.

Yellow: Caution—slow down and hold your position.

Red: Stop immediately—there is a serious wreck or the track is blocked.

Black: Pull into the pit area for inspection.

Blue with yellow stripe: Move over — you are being passed by leaders.

White: One lap to go in the race.

Checkered: Finish.

Danger from Steering Wheels

In a crash, early drivers were in danger of being stabbed by sharp deadly splinters from the wood rim of their steering wheel.

A strong unbreakable wheel was needed. Many ideas were tried without success. Finally an ingenious mechanic hit on a new idea.

He cut the teeth off the outer rim of a circular saw blade, traced on its face four spokes and a round hub, and cut them out. He then wrapped the outer edge with heavy tape and bolted his creation to the steering shaft of his racer.

The saw-blade was the answer. Strong and flexible, it had no breakable parts to injure the driver in a crash.

Such wheels were made for years. Today factory steering wheels for racers still follow the same flat, four-spoke style.

One-Handed Victory

Vibration in a race car can cause great discomfort and grave internal problems to a driver's body. Early drivers bound themselves as tightly as possible from waist to armpits with wide bandages. Later they covered the bandages with heavy tape.

Modern race cars are not so hard on the human system, but they are still punishing. Jim Rathman, after winning the Indy 500 in 1960, admitted he did not know what he'd have done if the race had been 15 minutes longer.

A creeping numbness had been overcoming his body. It had worked its way up to his arms. Only by steering with one hand and resting the other was he able to drive the final miles.

Track observers along each straightaway had observed Rathman changing driving hands and vigorously shaking the other as he roared by at well over 150 mph!

Racing Tires

The tires on a family car must have good tread to be safe for driving. The tread, or groove pattern, increases traction on wet roads.

In auto racing safe tires are vital. They vary in style according to the special requirements, but almost all are extra wide for better gripping.

Tires used by dirt track racers have deep, crosscut grooves in their face. The deep tread is important because it actually "bites" into the dirt surface as the car races around the track. Without this tread, the racer would slip and slide.

Cars racing on paved tracks use a much different tire. There is *no tread* at all across the wide, smooth face of their tires! Engineers have found that a flat design is the best for traction when racing on a perfectly dry paved track. A racer with such tires, called "slicks," is uncontrollable on a wet pavement however.

Up in the Air

Bobby Johns was leading the 1960 Daytona 500-mile race. He had four miles to go and his closest challenger was far behind. The race was his or so it seemed.

As he drove off the number two turn and headed down the long backstretch at over 150 mph, his 4,000-pound Pontiac racer was lifted completely off the track and sent spinning into the infield grass. What happened? A tire blowout? Did Johns lose control of the car? No, nothing that simple.

Air pressure had popped the rear window out of his car. The suction created by the wide opening actually hurled his car 60 feet through the air! Johns was uninjured but the unscheduled flight cost him the race.

Winner's Drink

The traditional victory drink of winners of the Indy 500 is milk!

Watch the event on TV. You will see the lucky winner given a bottle of milk while he is still in his car. Most drivers, thirsty and tired, down the milk eagerly. But there have been a few nonmilk drinkers who simply took a sip to maintain tradition.

Gilhooley

In auto racing slang you will hear the cry "Gilhooley!" It is the term given to a wild spin—the result of poor driving, a slick track, or tire failure. The term was coined in early racing days when a madcap driver, Tom Gilhooley, was competing.

Gilhooley was one of those drivers who was long on nerve, but short on ability. He was forever losing control of his racer and addling his brains in spins. His kind is still in action today, endangering others with spins, crashes, and erratic driving.

The next time you see a driver lose control and spin across the track, turn to your friend and say, "Wow, that was a real Gilhooley!"

Can This Record Be Broken?

They say records are set to be broken, but one that seems safe was set by race car driver, Ralph DePalma.

DePalma compiled a lifetime victory record of 2,757 wins in 2,886 starts.

That's a batting average of .950!

The Loneliest 500

The Indy 500 is the largest single sporting event in the world for attendance. Each year over 300,000 fans are at the speedway. Do you know what the second largest is? The prerace time trials!

Yet there was once a 500-mile event run on the Indy oval with not a single spectator in the stands!

The run was made in the winter of 1945. Firestone Rubber Company got permission to test a new synthetic rubber tire at the big track. A single race car was fitted with the new tires and driven by Wilbur Shaw.

The test was staged as a regular race, with pit stops and officials timing each lap. The tires performed very well, going the full 500 miles at over 100 mph without a change.

It was a numbing five degrees above zero that day. Shaw said it was the toughest 500 he had ever driven. "It seemed like five thousand miles!" he declared after the final lap.

"It's a Duesey"

The old expression, "It's a Duesey," stems from the high standards of quality set by the Duesenberg brothers, Fred and August, in building automobiles.

Made from 1920 to 1937, Duesenbergs had the best materials, the finest engineering, the most luxurious appointments, and price tags to match —$6,500 to $25,000. Today the cars command even higher prices from antique automobile collectors.

If you hear the expression, "It's a Duesey," you will know the speaker is heaping praise on something.

The Brickyard

The Indianapolis Speedway is a slightly banked, two and a half mile-oval track. It has two long straightaways of 5/8 of a mile each and four corners which, combined, measure the final one and a quarter miles.

The original dirt surface of 1909 did not hold up. In 1910 it was paved with over *three million* 10-pound bricks, each laid by hand.

Although the bricks were topped with a smooth asphalt in 1935, the track still retains its nickname, "The Brickyard."

About the Author

On August 27, 1954, a program of auto races was staged in Miami, Florida, to help raise money to fight a polio epidemic that was then sweeping the country. Al Powell, a leading racing car driver, was among those who volunteered their services for the benefit.

Although he was ill, suffering from severe back pains and headache, Al finished in second place that night. Later his illness was diagnosed. Al had polio, and he became permanently paralyzed — a quadraplegic.

Today, with the help of his wife, Betty Ruth, and their four children, Al maintains an active business and family life. The material for this fascinating book has come from his own experiences and those of his many friends throughout the racing world.